Don't Touch my Priv
I am a Child

CW00421111

Manyi Anabor

FJORD INDEX

Bessem rolled on the bed and laughed as Tony tickled her. They loved playing the Tickling game. They were excited because Grandpa was coming over to visit.

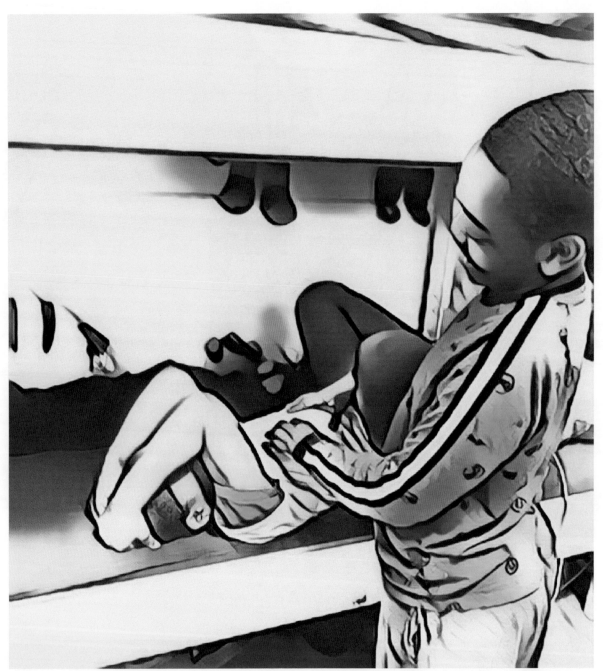

"Stop, Tony!" Bessem blurted out as she tried to stop laughing. Mama came into the bedroom.

"Tony, if she says stop, you should stop tickling her," Mama said.

Tony grumbled, "Mama, we were just playing, and it was Bessem who wanted to play the Tickling game."

"I could see that you were playing. But you must respect a person's wishes if they don't want to play anymore," Mama said.

"But Mama, she was laughing, which means she was having fun," Tony said.

"Tony, **Stop** means stop. And **No** means no, even when you think the other person is having fun," Mama said.

Tony was not happy. He stormed out of the room.

"Bessem, are you okay?" Mama said.

Bessem said, "No, I'm sad."

"Why are you sad?" Mama asked.

"Because Tony is upset about tickling me," she said.

Mama put her arms around her.

"He is not upset with you. He is annoyed because I told him to stop tickling you," Mama said.

Bessem said, "At first I wanted him to tickle me, but later on, I wanted him to stop, but I could not stop laughing."

"I understand. And well done for speaking up. You must always say **Stop** if you don't like something."

She nodded and they both smiled. Mama went to Tony's room and found him mumbling to himself about Mama treating him unfairly.

"Mama, it wasn't even my fault," Tony said.

"Tony, I am not blaming you for anything. I am aware that Bessem asked you to tickle her," Mama said, "When you were playing, did she tell you to stop tickling her?"

"She said I should stop but she was still laughing," Tony said.

"No matter how much fun you are having with your sister, your friends or anyone else, if they tell you they don't want to play anymore, you must stop immediately," Mama said.

Mama saw that he was still upset so she sat with him.

"Let me ask you a question," Mama said, "In school would you let anyone open your school bag and use your items without asking you?"

"No," he said.

"Why not?" Mama asked.

"Because they are my things, so they have to ask me first," he retorted.

Mama nodded, "What about if you were tired in school, and your friends suddenly started tickling you?"

"I would tell them to leave me alone," he said.

"They are your friends. Why would you tell them to leave you alone?" Mama asked him.

"Because I don't want to be tickled at that time."

Mama nodded, "If you are not in the mood, it is not okay for anyone to tickle you, regardless of whether it's me, your sister, your friends or anyone else."

Tony thought to himself, '*That is probably how Bessem felt earlier.*'

"Mama, I feel bad that I continued tickling Bessem when she said I should stop," he said.

"It's okay, the most important thing is to always make sure you respect people's boundaries, by respecting their wishes," Mama said.

Tony felt enlightened.

Just then, the doorbell rang. Mama went to see who was at the door.

"It is probably Grandpa," she smiled.

Grandpa came in with a warm smile as usual.

"Welcome, Papa! How was your journey?" Mama asked.

"Thank you, I had a good trip. How are you? Where are my favourite grandchildren?" he said as he looked over at Bessem who was beaming from ear to ear.

"My beautiful granddaughter, where is my giant hug?" he said, smiling.

"Hello Grandpa," Bessem said softly, as she was still upset from earlier.

"I know you love Grandpa's hugs," he urged as he leaned forward to hug her.

"Bessem, do you not want to hug Grandpa?" Mama asked.

"Not yet," she said shyly.

"That's alright," Mama said.

Bessem waved, "Hi Grandpa."

"Hello, my most beautiful and intelligent granddaughter!" he smiled.

Mama said, "Well done for not hugging when you didn't feel like it."

"It's alright if you don't want to give me a hug," Grandpa said, "Your mother is correct, I should have asked if you wanted a hug or not, instead of telling you to give me a hug."

Tony dashed into the room and was delighted to see Grandpa.

"Grandpa!" Tony ran over and hugged him.

Grandpa laughed, "What a warm welcome, Tony, you have grown tall! How is school?"

"It's okay," Tony said.

"And how is that your Maths teacher who you don't like because he gives a lot of homework?" Grandpa said, smiling.

"He no longer teaches in our school; he has gone to further his studies," Tony explained.

"That's good," said Grandpa, "so he can come back with more knowledge to share.

Tony looked thrilled as he looked down at the bag Grandpa had brought.

"Grandpa are these the books you promised to bring?"

"Yes, have a look at them and tell me which one you will read first," Grandpa chuckled.

Tony rifled through the books eagerly.

Mama noticed that Bessem had quietly left the room when Tony came in. Mama went and found Bessem sitting in a corner in her room.

"Are you okay?" Mama said.

Bessem said, "Is Grandpa happy because Tony hugged him?"

Mama said, "Grandpa loves you and Tony very much, regardless of whether you hugged him or not. Grandpa understands that we don't always feel like giving hugs. And that's okay."

"Does Grandpa sometimes not want to give hugs too?" Bessem asked.

Mama smiled, "Would you like to ask him yourself?"

Bessem dashed off excitedly, and Mama joined them later.

Mama said, "Bessem, how else could you have let Grandpa know you didn't want a hug?"

"Could I have said, 'I don't want a hug?'" Bessem said.

"That's a very good answer!" Grandpa said.

Mama smiled at Bessem proudly, "You must always say **No** if you don't want a hug. And this doesn't only apply to hugs. If someone touches you in a way you don't like, you should tell them to stop.

Bessem looked puzzled.

"How can someone touch me in a way I don't like?"

"That is a really good question," said Mama, "If someone touches you and it makes you feel uncomfortable. Or if they touch a part of your body which they should not touch… like your private parts. Do you remember the private parts?"

Bessem tried to remember.

"Penis for boys and vagina for girls," Tony said promptly, without looking up from the book he was reading.

"Well done, Tony," Grandpa seemed impressed.

"Bessem did you hear what Tony said?" Mama asked.

"Penis and vagina," she said.

Mama then pointed at Bessem's chest.

"What about these private parts here; what are they called?"

"Chest!" Bessem shouted.

"Good attempt but think of another word."

Mama pointed at her chest again, first to the left then to the right.

"Boobies!" Bessem blurted out.

Mama smiled, "Some people call them boobies but the correct name for them is breasts."

"Ah yes!" Bessem exclaimed.

Mama said to Bessem, "It is okay if you forgot the name. From now on, we will use the correct names of all the private parts, to help you remember them."

Tony whispered, "Is breast not a bad word?"

"No, breast is not a bad word. It is the correct name for that private part, and because it is private, no one else is allowed to see it or touch it. But it is not a bad word." Mama said.

"Okay," Tony said.

Mama continued, "It is the same thing with *vagina* and *penis*. Some people teach their children that these are bad words, when instead, it is important to use these words so children can learn to talk more freely about them."

Grandpa nodded.

He said, "Tony, I know you are a bit older now and children your age sometimes play inappropriate games which involve touching or showing body parts to one another. No matter what games you play with your friends, remember that we always play with our clothes on, and private parts are kept private."

"Okay," Tony answered.

"Good boy," Grandpa smiled.

"Can you name any other private parts?" Mama said.

Bessem and Tony looked down at each other trying to figure out other private parts.

"I can't remember!" Bessem said with exasperation.

Mama tried to help them out. She said, "You are sitting on it."

"Buttocks!" they both exclaimed.

Grandpa applauded them, "Very smart children."

They smiled.

"Mama, I remember there is another private part but I can't remember what it is." Tony said, as he looked over his body.

Mama said, "I'll give you a clue. It is the opening where poo comes out from. Who remembers what it's called?"

Bessem turned around attempting to look at her back.

"I didn't know that was a private part," she muttered.

"Yes," Mama smiled, "It's called the anus."

"Now I remember they taught us in school, but some children in my class said their parents said anus is a dirty word," Bessem said.

Mama explained, "Anus is not a dirty word. Some people just feel uncomfortable to say it, so they say it's a dirty word."

"Why do some people feel uncomfortable to say *anus*?" Bessem asked.

"Some people feel uncomfortable because when they were children, they were taught not to talk about their private parts. But nowadays, we know that it is better for children to use the correct names of their private parts, so that if they ever get hurt or touched on their private parts, they can tell someone which specific body part it was," said Mama.

Bessem seemed confused.

Mama continued, "I'll explain what I mean. The buttocks, breast, anus, penis and vagina are your private parts. The reason why they are called private parts is because they are meant only for you. No one else is allowed to see them."

Bessem and Tony nodded.

Mama continued, "No one is allowed to **see** your private parts, no one is allowed to **touch** them, or **take pictures** of them, and it is wrong for anyone to ask you to look at, or touch someone else's private parts. If anyone ever touches your private parts, or if they show you their private parts, you should tell me or your father immediately."

"Yes Mama," they said in unison.

"Also, if anyone puts their hand under your skirt, under your dress, or inside your trousers, or if they touch your private parts over your clothes, that is wrong. Tell me or your father if that ever happens. But if you are not able to tell us, who else can you tell?" Mama asked.

"Grandpa!" they shouted excitedly.

Grandpa smiled and said, "And if you are not able to tell any of us, you should tell other grownups until someone does something about it."

They nodded.

"Mama, will you be upset if someone touches our private parts?"
Bessem asked.

"That's a very intelligent question, Bessem. Grownups and older children know that it is wrong to touch a child's private parts. So, if they do so, it is wrong. And it is never a child's fault, no matter what. So, I will be very proud of you for telling me," Mama said.

"My dear grandchildren," Grandpa said, "Usually when an adult touches a child's private parts, they would ask the child to keep it a secret and not to tell anyone. There should be no secrets. If anyone tells you not to tell your parents something, make sure you tell your parents."

Tony asked, "If someone was trying to touch my penis, how can I tell them not to, without making them upset?"

"You should say, 'Don't touch my penis, I am a child.' Or 'Don't touch my vagina, I am a child.' Whether it is a teacher, a neighbour, a relative or a family friend, and even if they have been nice to you, tell them, 'Don't touch my private parts, I am a child," Mama said.

Bessem looked worried.

"Mama, what will happen to me if someone touched my private parts?"

"That is an amazing question, Bessem. There are so many sad things that can happen to a child when someone touches their private parts. It can affect the way in which the child's mind grows. It can make them feel very sad, a lot of the time. It can make them feel alone and sometimes find it difficult to make friends. It can make a child to feel like they are not worth anything, and they might not even like themselves. Many children who go through this sometimes have problems falling asleep at night because they keep having nightmares for many years, and during the day sometimes, some children have anxiety attacks because they are scared that bad things might happen to them," Mama said.

Grandpa noticed how closely they were paying attention.

"We are teaching you about these things because when children go through this and become grownups, they usually continue experiencing these sad things your mother has mentioned. But we can try to prevent this from happening by always talking to one another and by doing our best to ensure that our private parts remain private, alright?" he said smiling.

"Yes, Grandpa, thank you, Grandpa," they hugged him.

Advice to Caregivers on Child Abuse Prevention

There is no guaranteed way to protect a child from sexual abuse. But there are things you can do to reduce the risk of this happening.

1. Arm your child with knowledge that might keep them safe.
2. Speak to your child about private parts early. Use actual names for private parts. For instance, vagina not *bumbum*.
3. Teach them that having private parts means no one is allowed to see, touch or take pictures of them. And no one is allowed to tell them to touch another person's private parts.
4. Teach them that body secrets are not allowed.
5. Listen to a child and always believe them.
6. Teach the child that if someone wants to touch their private parts, they should say they need the bathroom, so they can leave the room.
7. Monitor the child's caregiver (teacher, private tutor, baby-sitter, house help, relative or family friend) and ask the child regularly about the conversations they have with them.

FJORD INDEX

ISBN: 9798376184721
Imprint: Independently Published

Printed in Great Britain
by Amazon

38296508R00016